# VILLAGE GHETTOLAND

## VOLUME 1

H. Monte

M
MACK MEDIA

For Moms

For Pops

For Maxine

For those focused on capturing lions rather than mice

# FAMILY FIRST

---

## MEET THE PARENTS

### MARVIN

**Marvin Mack**, "Pops", is a steadfast man of few words but he possesses an abundance of principles and resolute loyalty to his family.  Pops moves slowly as if each step is calculated and to a certain extent, they are.  He taught his boys the importance of respect and would always make the distinction between demanding respect and earning it. 'Be slow to speak and quick to listen…your mouth will get you in trouble but your eyes and ears will get you out of it…' are lessons that he would instill in his boys ad nauseam. You see, because Marvin did not have education beyond the tenth grade, he earned his degree on the streets of Anderson, where he graduated cum laude. Six months before his seventeenth birthday, Marvin became a father when Melvin was born and within the next four years, he and Pam got married and had a second son, Randy. Marvin was thrusted into the deep end of life's cesspool by his circumstances and in the name of survival and financial security for his growing family, he adapted an American pastime– illegal trade.  In 1989, Marvin was employed with the Anderson, NJ sanitation department; however, during the 1970s, he supplied marijuana, heroin, and cocaine throughout Northern New Jersey and Manhattan.  'Money Marv…', as he was affectionately called, '...was a bad mothafucka back in the day!' Melvin would often remind us when he thumbed through old photos or reminisced about the ad hoc shopping sprees with Marvin to Delancey Street that he would go on as a younger child.  Despite the negative perception associated with dealing drugs, Marvin's efforts were not futile.  In 1980, during Pam's pregnancy with Monte, their third child, Marvin purchased a home for his wife, children and mother to live in; the American Dream realized!  Though Monte was not proud of many of his father's decisions, he appreciated the sacrifices he made for his family and loved him unconditionally.

# <u>PAM</u>

**Pamela Mack** was the household matriarch and queen of the pack.  She was soft spoken but firm.  She was generous beyond belief and was respected as the second mother to most of her sons' neighborhood friends (and girlfriends).  But do not be fooled by her saint-like tendencies because though she leads with respect for all mankind, when she is forced to protect herself and her family, she is fierce and unforgiving.  Legend has it that before the birth of Monte, a former colleague of Pam's, named Molly, committed the carnal sin of pointing a finger in Pam's face and consequently, got her ass kicked in return.  At home, whenever Pam demonstrates frustration, to tease her, Randy would often say, "Uh oh- MOLLY, RUN!"  Pam was born in the South.  She was always hospitable and very scrupulous; however, for her family, she made exceptions and remained unconditionally loyal.  Pam and Marvin have been a unit since they were teenagers and during their time together, she has been everything from his designated driver to his consigliere.  Figuratively speaking, she knew where the bodies were buried.  With Marvin's old way of life in the rear view, Pam worked as a civil servant with dreams of retiring and growing old with Marvin Down South.  Those dreams were perceived as realities until she discovered that her sons were destined to become new and improved models of Marvin– the dark side of Anderson, NJ was wrapping its arms tightly around her boys and she was forced to defer her dreams.

## THE MACK BROTHERS

## MONTE

On the surface, he is a virtuous child with a heart of gold. Soft spoken and a bit shy, Monte is a "momma's boy" that is a bit insecure about his speech impediment and stature. Monte is non-threatening to the general public; however, he has a sinister imagination that he often allows to play out in real life. Academically, Monte struggles but was forgiven for this flaw because of his disposition and the perception that he is the ideal young man with great potential and a bright future.  Although Monte's personality is different from Randy and Melvin, he is awestruck by his older brothers' unique ability to navigate danger.

# <u>RANDY</u>

**Randy is brilliant**- he is academically gifted, charismatic and analytical. However, Randy has a very aggressive side that Monte exploits when his mind gets running with ideas. Randy's intellectual gifts become his weaknesses when he allows boredom to motivate his deviance and opposition to authority. At such a young age, Randy's natural leadership qualities makes him a threat to those in search of maintaining order in school and out.

# <u>MELVIN</u>

**Melvin is the eldest** son and in his mind, he was the family underboss.  He was a spitting image of their father though, was a bit more vocal and definitely more ostentatious. Because Marvin and Pam were teenage parents, Melvin's experience was unique as he received the best (and worst) of both worlds.  Moreover, Marvin inadvertently taught him _everything_ that he knew. Melvin was a born hustler and he was well aware of it from an early age.  He was a solid student in school; however, his level of confidence was often mistaken for arrogance and insubordination that often led to conflict with school officials and subsequent punishment.

In the streets, Melvin was a diplomat- he made connections and nurtured relationships on behalf of Marvin and by the time Melvin finished the 8th grade, he had a small team of childhood friends with whom he established his own hand-to-hand marijuana operation down the street from their house on the corner of Liberty Ave.  As Marvin's son, Melvin and his "crew" got a pass from the older guys on Liberty and because of their youthfulness, they were perceived by the 'old heads' as a distraction rather than competition.  By 13, he did not earn enough to gain independence but it was enough to provide some financial relief to his parents, who had begun to transition onto a fixed budget as Marvin slowly stepped away from "the game".

# SCHOOL DAZE

*Splash!* **'Wake up, fat boy!** You pissed the bed again'
there was Monte's older brother, Randy, waking him up
with a cup of cold water to go along with the soaked sheets
left behind by yet another wet night.  "But I prayed on it
last night- this was not supposed to happen." he thought...
Oh well, here's to another morning shower that will surely

use up the limited amount of hot water in the house. 'Ma, you should start making him go to school smelling like pee- - I bet that would teach him not to piss at night...' Horrified at the thought of attending his new ALL WHITE school with his new ALL WHITE classmates accompanied by the aroma of urine, Monte quickly ran into the bathroom, locked the door by jamming it with a sock, and jumped into the shower.  This was the typical morning routine on school days but today was different because Monte's mother recently transferred him and Randy to another school district that was two towns over in the suburbs, or as Randy put it, 'WHITEYVILLE'.  Pam made the executive decision to move the boys to a new school because she was running out of options to give them a 'good education', a fair shot, and most importantly, an escape from the so-called 'trouble' that accompanied urban public school in their home city of Anderson, NJ, where the reputation of their older brother, Melvin, preceded them.  It was 1989- Monte was 8, Randy was 12 and Melvin was 16.

Sitting at the edge of the bed, contemplating his outfit for his first day of school, Monte was torn between the gray Russel sweat suit or the new jeans that mom made for him on her sewing machine because the local Woolworth store did not carry acid wash jeans in a size that fit him. "Are you wearing your HUSKY jeans today, Meaty Monte?" asked Randy. Monte's mind was made up at that very moment- the sweat suit it will be because 'WHITEYVILLE' was not prepared for that amount of denim on the first day... If you have not already guessed it, Monte is overweight- a physical characteristic that gets him in as much trouble as it gets him out of. If Melvin needed an easy target to rehearse his fat jokes on, Monte was at the ready. Likewise, if Randy wanted permission to do something that would surely be denied, he'd say 'Hey fat boy, go ask mommy..." Monte was always amenable to his older brothers' commands. In fact, Monte was compliant to almost everyone. Despite his inner emotions, he kept the same grin on his face-- an expression that in his mind, communicated 'I love you' and 'fuck you' simultaneously.

As he jumped into his sweatpants, Monte could smell the aroma of fresh margarine squares melting on white toast as it broiled at the bottom of the oven. 'Hmm' he thought. Toast with butter and jelly was among his favorites but this morning was exceptional so his mother fried beef bacon to accompany the toast. Randy opted for his daily meal -a salad bowl full of Fruity Pebbles cereal. 'Time to go, Grandma Maxine is here to drive you losers to school!' yelled Melvin as he sat at the dining room table scrubbing one of his 20 pairs of sneakers with a toothbrush and dish soap. 'Couldn't hack it, had to pack it!' Melvin said sarcastically as they exited the apartment door. Though he did not have a say in the decision to transfer Monte and Randy out of the Anderson school district, Melvin did not support the move.  Because Melvin perceived survival in Anderson schools as a right of passage, the transfer was viewed as cowardly.  Yet, Monte perceived Melvin dropping out of school as equally cowardly. However, at eight years old, he admired and feared Melvin too much to defend mom with this argument.  Furthermore, Monte's 9th birthday is only a month away and Melvin already promised him a yellow Sony Sport Walkman and another pair of Reebok 5411 sneakers- 'don't block your blessing!' Monte's inner voice whispered as he ran for the front door. "See ya Mel" he said as he left the house.

Off they went. Today represented a crossroads not only for Monte and Randy but for Pam and Marvin as well because this ALL WHITE school had the potential to either broaden their horizons or minimize them. As they crossed the intersection where Anderson ends and Glen Park begins, they passed Monte's favorite donut shop. "PULL OVER!" he yelled while rubbing his belly. Assuming that Monte wanted to stop for a snack, he was ignored by everyone except Randy, who quipped, 'Ma, he's hungry AGAIN!' No response from Pam…"Please pull over" he repeated.

Monte was a respectful kid but if his back was against the wall and he had to defend himself, he could transform into a menace in an instant. "Stop the damn car so that I can go inside to take a shit!" he yelled. Grandma Maxine brought the car to a screeching halt and matched his verbal assault with one of her own- "if you're not going to show some respect, your fat ass will shit yourself and then walk to school!"... Randy nervously snickered and Monte retreated. 'I'm sorry, but I am really nervous about starting a new school and I need to use the bathroom. Can we please stop at the donut shop?" Grandma was a verbal assassin and all eleven of her grandchildren admired her for it. She tells it like it is and how it should be. Beyond that, the kids especially loved her because she occasionally granted them permission to use bad words.  During family events, as photos were taken, Grandma Maxine did not allow anyone to say 'cheese!' "BULLSHIT" was her go-to and somehow the smiles were always bigger and brighter. So needless to say that when Monte temporarily found himself in the cross hairs of the queen bee, he waved the white flag before things got ugly.

During the 80s, in Northern New Jersey, getting a 'good education' meant attending one of the tuition-based private or parochial schools within a neighboring town-- solutions that were not viable options for the Mack family to explore.

Access to resources was an absolute barrier until one Saturday night while sipping E&J and listening to the melodic notes Anita Baker *'Caught up in the Rapture';* Pam had a premonition to send them to school in Glen Park.  Pam had the wherewithal to understand that if her two younger sons would have a fighting chance, she would need to place them in an academic setting that was foreign. By the late 1990s, this practice of 'stealing education' was a commonality; however, in 1989, this shit was an innovation and Pam knew it!   What are the costs and benefits to placing young black boys in a learning environment where almost the entire population was white?  This question was at the center of a dilemma that many black families pondered but one that few black families were afforded the opportunity to explore.  Fortunately, for Monte and Randy, Grandma Maxine lived in the suburbs and they were exported to WHITEYVILLE to discover if there was any value in her location beyond a large backyard and an upstairs bedroom. Indeed, they were lucky to receive a chance for a "fresh start" and though Marvin remained skeptical of the proposed shift, he and Pam were committed to ensuring that this perceived privilege was not lost on their boys.

Stepping into the new school, Monte was immediately taken aback by the amount of light that entered the hallways.  As he thought to himself,  "It's sooo bright!", he could hear an echo of Randy's voice in his head saying "it's sooo white!".  'Welcome to Central School, Mont-ae; I'm Mr. Skimmer, your Principal" Mr. Skimmer wore white hair, had steel blue eyes and the tight-lipped grin that Monte was unable to read at that moment.  At any rate, Skimmer's posture led Monte to question the sincerity in his 'welcome' greeting.

In search of belonging, Monte experienced some trial and error as he tried to find a group for which he can identify with. However, navigating this new terrain would prove more difficult than expected.  Back home in Anderson, a shoulder bump accompanied by a light *your mother* joke would stamp his presence and gain him the attention required for survival. However, this was not Anderson- Monte was one of three Black students in the entire school and it was painfully apparent that playing 'the dozens' was not a pastime in Glen Park, NJ.

'Class, we have a new student, let us all give Mon-tay a big Central School welcome!' She completely mispronounced his name but at the moment, Monte accepted the error assuming that this population was not accustomed to such a name- he would later realize that these errors were becoming habitual and too coincidental to be unintentional- *'Welcome to Central School, Montaaaay'* the class repeated in unison. Monte timidly shuddered as he responded 'he-he hello'. He was deathly afraid of public speaking and hated being the center of attention. This encounter with his new class sent his nerves through the roof and that familiar sensation from a car ride with grandma was beginning to revisit *him...'please don't fart, please don't fart...'* he begged himself as he walked to his desk. Bowels intact, he survived the journey to his seat. Following the awkward yet brief introduction, the teacher continued her lesson as Monte pretended to pay attention as he imagined what his new school was serving for lunch that day. Nevertheless, as he surveyed the classroom and observed the sea of pink faces, Monte took a deep breath and smiled because he thought of Pam's sacrifice to place him in a new school- he was overwhelmed with hope daydreaming about the possibilities for this new setting.

Monte paused his daydreaming to focus on the lesson just in case he was challenged by the teacher and called upon to answer a question. Fortunately, he was spared from enduring further anxiety but much to his surprise, the level of work was no more challenging than what he experienced in his Anderson school.  During class, he could not help but notice, through his peripheral vision, blank stares from his classmates, who appeared to be sizing him up.  Perhaps this was their attempt to engage with him or maybe his presence made them uncomfortable and they did not want him there, he thought. Regardless, Monte was optimistic and chose to see the situation positively, convincing himself that they were admiring his features rather than admonishing them.

The bell rang signaling lunch time and Monte was eager to participate in his first Central School dining experience.  He was quick to his feet as he made his way to the exit, despite not having a clue of where the lunchroom was located.  He lined up behind the teacher and waited patiently for directions.  While standing in line, he was approached by one of his new classmates who rather than introduce himself, said "where are you from?" Monte was a little nervous as this was his first direct interaction within the new school.  However, a true product of Anderson, Monte initially interpreted the student's inquiry as a check on what neighborhood he represented. In such cases, the reply would be "I'm from Liberty Ave, *where you from?*" but this was not Anderson and he was posing as a Glen Park resident so in his most non-threatening tone, he toed the party line that he rehearsed with Pam the night before- "I live in town with my grandparents" he replied. Monte then inched closer to the exit, signaling to the inquisitive classmate that he was disinterested in answering his questions.

Upon reaching the cafeteria, Monte was immediately taken aback by the buffet style arrangement, which was very different from the limited selections of tuna and Salisbury steak offered at his previous school district. He anxiously perused the lunch options as he inhaled the collection of aromas that filled the air.  Monte had a large appetite and an intense attraction to the familiar flavors associated with chicken nuggets and french fries that stared back at him from behind the aluminum serving tray. However, it was the first day of school and he was desperate to fit in with his classmates.  Therefore, to avoid fulfilling the prophecy of the *fat, black kid from the hood who loves fried food*, he selected the meal that he observed on the trays of most students- a plain bagel with cream cheese and grape jelly! The ingredient combination was foreign to Monte's palate however; he prepared himself to eat the meal anyway.  During lunch, he sat quietly among his classmates as they chatted about soccer practice and weekends at the Jersey Shore.  Just as he began to imagine what Randy was experiencing at Glen Park Junior High, Monte felt a tap on his shoulder. It was a short boy eating a ham sandwich and wearing a plaid shirt. Monte peaked his eyes up away from his meal and said "hello". The boy, staring intently, responded with "Hi new kid- Can I touch your hair?"  Perplexed by the blatant display of covert bias, Monte shyly chuckled and asked the boy to repeat himself; he heard him clearly the first time but Monte needed a moment to craft a proper response. So the boy in the plaid shirt audaciously repeated his request to touch Monte's hair and as he bit into his ham sandwich, Monte said, "maybe some other time- you're eating a ham sandwich and hands that touch swine, can never touch mine!" Monte used humor in an attempt to disarm the boy while regaining some confidence– he was less interested in fitting in at this point. Following his reply, it was a moment of awkward silence before the boy began to laugh hysterically. "Good one, New Kid! That was pretty funny," the boy said as he playfully slapped Monte on the back and returned to his seat. Soon afterwards, the "lunch lady" announced that it was time for recess and Monte followed the herd of students to the playground.

Recess at Central School was similar to his previous school in Anderson. It was organized confusion- students ran around aimlessly while others walked the perimeter to gossip. However, one notable difference was the absence of the ever-present threat of a schoolyard fight breaking out. Beyond the typical conflicts that can arise during an intense game of kickball, there were no signs of imminent violence or bullies with names like "Stacks" (*another story for another day*). Monte intended to use his recess time for observation and learning the lay of the land; however, before he had the opportunity to embark on his discovery mission, the boy from the lunchroom in the plaid shirt approached him with yet another inappropriate request. "Hey New Kid, we need another player on the court- you're a good basketball player aren't you?" Monte parted his lips to decline when the student interjected with "*of course you are*- let's go!" Monte obliged, despite basketball not being his strong suit.

Luckily for Monte, lunch recess did not allow enough time for extensive play so he did not run the risk of becoming a sweaty mess.  On the basketball court, Monte's greatest attribute was his body mass so he just stood in the way of his opponents and let his teammates do the rest.  As the bell rang to bring recess to an end, someone passed Monte the ball and yelled 'New Kid take the last shot!' In an instant, Monte dribbled the ball between his legs before tossing it up towards the hoop. It went in with a *swish* and the students on the court released a collective *Wooo!* Monte's impressive playground performance not only surprised him but also left a positive impression on his classmates. For the first time that day, Monte felt truly seen by his peers.

After recess, Monte made his way to the water fountain for a quick drink before going back to class.  As soon as the cold water touched his lips, he was refreshed. There was no presence of metallic notes hidden within the flavor of the water and the liquid was springing from the nozzle. Furthermore, Monte did not have to press his mouth on the dispenser to retrieve it! 'I can get used to this' he thought. Just as Monte began to lose himself in adoration for this twist on a familiar, often undesirable libation, he heard a small voice whisper "there's a black spider in our school...and he's drinking water" *Momma told me there would be days like this...* While this assault was not accompanied by the proverbial 'N-word' that he expected, he definitely recognized it as racial bias.  However, Monte did not have the language to eloquently describe this experience and contextualize it within the nuances of institutional racism.  Fortunately for him, he was armed with the wit and confidence of the overweight younger brother of his village- Anderson, New Jersey-  **'shut the fuck up!'** was his signature response and today he did not hesitate to deploy it. Silence fell over the corridor as everyone on the water line gasped.  Monte held his breath and waited for a response but seeing the instantaneous transition in the girl's hue, from pink to bordeaux, signaled to Monte that he won that round.  This would be his first encounter with the dark side of his new white world but it would not be his last.

Meanwhile, in junior high school, Randy was having the time of his life! What Pam viewed as an opportunity for positive change, the operative word for Randy was 'opportunity'. On Randy's first day, he linked up with Caleb, the only other Black 7th grader who, essentially, was the suburban version of Randy.  This created a win-win situation for Randy, as he was able to expand his charismatic influence while recruiting a partner in crime- *literally*. With Caleb by his side, Randy wreaked havoc.

h. monte: village ghetto land

2

## BOOGIE IN YOUR BUTT

**It is finally here!** Monte and Randy awaited this day for weeks. Tonight is the night of the Ashford and Simpson concert that Pam and Marvin have been planning for months.

As they made their way toward the door, Pam gathered her sons to deliver marching orders- "Boys, behave yourself while we're out. No company and no fighting...Food is on the stove and I left ten dollars on the dresser for emergencies…" Marvin chimed in with one of his signature one-liners, "Your big brother is up the street and the boxing gloves are in the closet" translation: *settle your differences before we get home...*

After the door slammed shut, Monte ran to the front window to make sure he saw Marvin's Pontiac Firebird pull away from the house.

"What do you want to do, Randy?" Monte asked with a twinkle in his eye that suggested he expected pure anarchy.  'Don't even think about it- we **<u>ARE NOT</u>** ordering Chinese food, Fat Ass!' Randy assumed Monte was referring to dinner. However, Monte was anticipating having the house to themselves and having fun.  Though Melvin was just up the block, on Liberty Ave, and Marvin's mother, Grandma Rose, lived in the downstairs apartment, they were independent for the next few hours.

Typically, when Pam needed short term supervision for the boys, Grandma Rose would periodically call upstairs for proof of life.  However, she had reliable hearing in only one ear so the boys would pretty much have to set off an explosion for her to be alarmed. Legend has it that twenty years prior, Grandma Maxine, aided by some Kentucky bourbon and a Black women's pride, is to blame for her hearing loss.  However, Randy is Monte's primary source for this tale so the claim, while provocative, is definitely questionable.

"Let's throw old sneakers at the stray cats in the backyard...Do we still have the BB gun? Let's play on the phone...come on Randy- let's tear shit up!" said Monte.

Before Randy could reply, Monte was already digging in Marvin's crate of vinyl albums.  "What are you looking for, Monte?" Randy asked. "You'll see..." Monte replied.  After a few moments, Monte emerged holding an album sleeve with none other than the king himself, Eddie Murphy, wearing a red flower in his afro and a smile that, in Monte's mind, said "*let's tear shit up*"...

For the next three hours, Monte and Randy exhausted themselves with everything from pillow fighting, marathon games of Mario Brothers on Nintendo, prank calling the local restaurants and arm wrestling. They searched for the BB gun but were unsuccessful so they made slingshots with wire hangers to shoot off the back porch at trespassing cats.  With no adults in sight, they relished the freedom to make (and break) their own rules, albeit temporarily.

Out of boredom, Monte made a "syrup sandwich" and although this snack disgusted Randy, he challenged Monte to eat it as fast as possible.  They soon realized that they were laughing with one another more than they were arguing.  They took a break from their shenanigans in their parents' room and decided to watch music videos that Melvin recorded on the VCR the day before.  Music was a big part of the Mack house-- no one in the family was a musician but they all loved to sing and dance, sometimes for better, sometimes for worse.

As the videos played, the boys repeated the lyrics and pretended they were performers. This was especially true when the video for Big Daddy Kane's "Warm it up, Kane" appeared on the screen!

The boys quickly jumped to their feet in an attempt to keep up with dance moves. They kicked and spinned for two minutes before they crashed onto the floor gasping for air. "Kane is the greatest ", Monte said in between his labored breathing.  "Yea he's pretty cool..." Randy replied.

"...Hey, Fat Boy, I got an idea- you want a hairstyle like Kane's?" Absolutely! Monte replied. OK- go get the clippers and meet me in the kitchen.

Apprehensive about Randy's ability to give him a cool haircut, Monte fetched the clippers and entered the mirror-free kitchen full of enthusiasm. The boys were excited engage in a new activity that was presumably constructive and non-sinister.

Randy was grinning from ear-to-ear as his eyes followed the clippers gliding over Monte's head.  Signaled by Randy's expression, Monte's excitement grew as he anticipated his fresh haircut; he was prematurely beginning to plan his outfit for the next school day when suddenly, he heard a snap. 'What the fuck was that, Randy?' Monte said. "The razor guard fell off as I was making your banana part" Randy nervously replied.  Monte accepted his response however he remained clueless of what that actually meant for the outcome of this haircut.

"Now I have to fix it but don't worry" Randy's voice trembled as he attempted to reassure Monte that all was well. On the contrary, Randy was shitting bricks. Unbeknownst to Monte, the clipper malfunction caused Randy to veer to the left and Monte's coveted banana part was now bifurcated.  After a moment of deliberating within his own head, Randy whispered to himself, "I got it" 'Hey, Fats, banana parts are played out- lets be original...I'm giving you a part shaped like an arrow instead"

As the *baby boy* of the family, his older brothers always enamored Monte.  From fashion ideas to slang words, Monte observed the moves they made and though they would often remind him not to follow their paths, he admired them to no end.

Given this fact, if Randy told him that he was giving him a 'cool' haircut, Monte did not give his advice a second thought.

After about 15 minutes of head tilting followed by pinches from the clippers, Randy nervously held a small mirror up to Monte and said, "What ya think, its nice right?"

When Monte laid eyes on the 2-inch wide arrow that was in the center of his head, he paused and inhaled all of the air his lungs would allow and grinned. *"MOTHAFUCKER, YOUR DAYS ARE NUMBERED...if I don't kill you, mommy and daddy will!"* This was the rage-filled response that his inner voice delivered; however, on the outside, Monte held his head high and submitted to Randy's will with a reluctant sigh and a cynical "it's a dope haircut, Randy- *Thanks Big Bro*!"

There was no music playing at the time but all Monte could hear in the back of his mind were the melodic notes of Eddie Murphy's "Boogie in your Butt" Perhaps it is because he anticipated the inevitable ass whipping that his parents would surely deliver...

"Wet your hair and let me brush it for you," Randy said in an attempt to salvage the damage.  Annoyed by the lack of innovation, "What will that do?" Monte asked.  "It will give you waves..." Randy replied.  Annoyance quickly transitioned to insult as Monte realized that in that moment, Randy was mistaking his amenability for weakness -

*Marvin told me there would be days like this*- "Nigga, don't play me!" Monte yelled.

"...You want me to believe that this shit looks good? You cannot talk yourself out of this one, big bro! We are dead when Mommy and Daddy get back home." Randy began sweeping up hair and Monte retreated to the bedroom to sit on the bottom bunk and reflect on the brief life he saw flash before his eyes in one short night.

From that point on, it seemed as if time was flying by. The living room felt like a Death Watch Area and Eddie Murphy's "*Hit by a Car*" was beginning to sound like a prophecy.

Despite Monte's disdain for his new look and Randy's shame in disappointing his younger brother, the boys were bonded in their shared fear of their parents' imminent wrath when they arrived home. "What do you think they will do, Randy?" Monte asked. "I don't know but don't worry..." Randy responded with uncertain bravery. "Let's tell them that----" Monte's words were interrupted by the sound of the entry door opening followed by creaking footsteps coming up the carpet-less staircase in the hallway.

Monte and Randy turned to one another as if it was the last time they would see one another (*similar to the separation of Seely and Netty in <u>The Color Purple</u>*).

They held their breath in unison and waited for the door to open.  Monte's inner track star tried convincing him that he can outrun the inevitable danger but his outer, more realistic conscience reminded him that his body mass will fail him in this endeavor.  So he just waited alongside Randy and settled for the ass whipping.

While keys jingled as the lock's inner mechanisms shifted to unbolt the door, Monte closed his eyes and braced himself for impact.

Finally, the door swung open and he heard "MOVE ASSHOLES, I HAVE TO USE THE BATHROOM" it was Melvin taking a "break" from his shift on Liberty Ave to appear responsible by checking in on his younger brothers just before their parents returned.

As he pushed his way past Randy and Monte, he could not help but notice the arrow shaved into Monte's scalp. "Awww shit!" He said. "...what happened???"

'Fatboy wanted a haircut' was Randy's response.  'Okay but what the hell did you do? And WHY the hell does it look like a street sign?'

"The clipper guard broke so I had to improvise," Randy said.  *Improvise*? Man, is that the best you can come up with? *HAHAHAHAHAHA*-- Mommy and Daddy are going to kick some ass tonight!'

Melvin's commentary added an element of angst that was uninvited by the boys.  Monte fought back tears while attempting to be a stand up co-defendant to Randy but then they heard the steps creak- AGAIN. This time the creaking was accompanied by a light melodic humming of Ashford and Simpson's *'Ain't no mountain high enough*- it was Marvin!

"Quick- put these hats on,' Melvin yelled as he shoved two of his suede Kangol hats into their hands and ran into the bathroom. It was a desperate attempt to buy his little brothers some time and in the absence of a better idea, they put the Kangols on and greeted their father at the door as if nothing was awry.

Nevertheless, given Marvin's street smarts and "hood IQ", he saw through the bullshit before the boys could open their mouths. "What's up, Pops? How was the concert?" Randy said. In true Marvin fashion, he withheld his reaction to the awkwardness and pretended as if his sons standing before him shirtless wearing suede hats at 11pm was common. "The concert was great- your mother loved it"

Marvin was strategic. Though he was unaware of the situation, he remained composed. Whatever the issue was, he wanted the boys to resolve their own problems "*like men*". Besides, he knew that Pam would surely discover what caused the boys to act so mysteriously.

Monte and Randy were relieved that Marvin bypassed their appearance; however, they both knew that Pam would not extend the same level of grace. Suddenly, as the door swung open, they heard "*SOLID!...Solid as a rock rock rock...*" there was Pam, singing, dancing and glowing like a newlywed at a wedding reception.

The combination of civil service employment and the full-time job of raising three boys in Anderson, New

Jersey did not afford Pam and Marvin the opportunity for quality time with one another so this night was extraordinary.

'Tonight was perfect, boys- the concert was great, dinner was excellent and your father actually danced! Can you believe it?' The thought of knowing that Pam's adrenaline would soon tailspin out of control, was too much for Monte to bear and he crumbled under duress- "MA, LOOK AT THIS SHIT!"--Monte snatched off his Kangol only to reveal the huge arrow part on his head.

'What happened to *ride or die*, Fat boy?' Randy exclaimed.

Monte succumbed to the pressure of Pam's disappointment, turned 'State's witness' and re-assigned his role from *willing participant* to *victim*. Realizing that Pam's fury was forthcoming, Randy stiffened his shoulders and nervously held his head high as he said 'it was an accident, Ma. Blame me- my bad...' overhearing Randy's response, Marvin grinned with pride but on the contrary, Pam growled with pain.

'Go get the extension cord…THE BRAIDED ONE!' In the Mack household, Pam's weapon of choice corresponded to the degree of sons' offense and the severity of the punishment she would deliver: (1) the switch, a thin branch from the outside bush, was for minor infractions, (2) the belt was for misdemeanors and (3) the standard extension core was reserved for felonies. However, if Pam had to break glass for the *braided* extension cord, she was going nuclear and even Grandma Rose would be able to hear the cries from Randy.

Absolved and out of harm's way as he sat on the toilet, Melvin chuckled and yelled 'Molly run!' from behind the bathroom door.

"Ma, it's not his fault!' Monte interjected in a last ditch effort to beg for Pam's mercy. "I respect your honesty but don't worry- you're next, baby!" was Pam's response.

Out of time, out of excuses and out of lifelines, both boys accepted fate and sobbed quietly. Randy slowly walked towards the closet to retrieve the extension cord while Monte walked towards the record player. He reached back into the crate of vinyl records, grabbed the 'TP' Teddy

Pendergrass album and put the needle on the one song that was fitting for the final dance of the evening..."Love T.K.O." it was a night to remember…

# FRIDAY NIGHT LIGHTS

**Despite his youth and perceived naiveté**, Monte's exposure to the exploits of his elders allowed him to be both a sponge and a wallflower.  His ability to observe his surroundings while taking inventory of his environment kept him out of trouble because he was aware of the figurative landmines and he knew how to avoid them.  He was just as mischievous as his peers were; however, he had mastered the art of doing the wrong shit, the right way- or at least he believed that to be the case.  By the time Monte turned 12, he saw his fair share of law enforcement and corrections facilities.  You name it- county jails, state prisons, juvenile detention centers, probation offices, rehab institutions and bail bondsmen were all destinations with which Monte was familiar.  If a badge or a full body search accompanied it, Monte navigated it because Pam would drag him with her everywhere in an attempt to break the cycles that were perverse within their family. Monte constantly received lectures from his father and older brothers on the importance of education and staying out of "trouble"; however, they were incapable of demonstrating just HOW to execute those plans. Notwithstanding Pam's 'scared straight' deterrent tactics, these environments often featured personnel that consistently made a point of verifying Monte's age and relation to Marvin, Melvin and Randy, as if they were anticipating him to take up residence at their "fine establishments" in the future.  Nevertheless, Pam did not shelter Monte from these realities and the potential future that awaited him if history repeated itself.

On one occasion, while Marvin, Pam and Monte were attending a court hearing for Melvin at the Anderson courthouse, as they walked through the lobby, Monte heard a booming voice of a man say "Mack!" This grabbed the attention of the whole family but after matching the voice with the pale face, they all knew the person they were talking to. "*WELL IF IT AINT MONEY MARV*!" the man said. It was Hugo, Anderson Police Department's most infamous narcotics detective- Hugo was admired by many and abhorred by many more. Hugo was a 6'3, 350lb white man with a baritone voice that has been etched in Monte's mind since the age of five. "Marv, you're making my job too easy- I did not expect you to come to me, I was expecting to pay you and your family a special visit again," Hugo said as he glanced at Monte and winked his left eye. The sight of Hugo made Monte sick to his stomach and the bubbles forming within his gut were reminiscent of his first day of school in Glen Park. "Ma, I don't feel well, I think I have to shit!" Monte whispered to Pam as she tried her best not to give Hugo the "Molly treatment" Pam was so incensed by the sight of Hugo along with his arrogance that she failed to notice Monte's use of bad language.

Meanwhile, Marvin was cool as a fan. Un-phased by what Hugo was implying, Marvin responded with some sarcasm of his own- "You're always welcome to visit, Hugo. Although, if you tell me in advance, I will arrange to have complimentary 'lines' (of cocaine) prepared for you and your team" Marvin's quip was accompanied by a wink to reciprocate Hugo's. Nervous laughter and blank stares fell over the faces of Hugo and his cronies in an instant. Marvin gently placed his arm around Monte's shoulder and guided him towards the restroom.  Once in the restroom, Marvin firmly grabbed Monte's hand and said "I know you remember that asshole but in anger or in fear, never reveal your emotions, son…" "But will he come back, Dad?" Monte asked with a look in eyes that almost shattered Marvin's soul. "**NO**!" Marvin fired back in frustration. Realizing that his tone rattled Monte further, he responded a second time- "no, my son" he repeated softly. With doubt in their eyes and hope in their hearts, Monte and Marvin stared at their reflections in the restroom mirror as they sought solace in one another.  However, as their imagination began to drift, it was evident that the ghosts of that past encounter continued to torment their family relentlessly.

It began as a typical Friday night during the fall of 1986- Randy and Monte finished bathing and ate dinner, all in time to catch their Friday TV shows.  They ran from the kitchen into the living room and sat down in front of the family's television positioned on the floor adjacent to their paneled glass entrance door.  The Mack family TV was a 300 pound, wood-grain RCA console model that served as furniture just as much as entertainment.  Pam did not watch TV much but she used it as both a bargaining chip and a mantle for picture frames and plants.  The Mack boys cherished this piece of furniture because it was their first color TV and they had a VCR. On each side of the monitor, were small wooden doors that housed VHS tapes and excess dust from the living room traffic. In their neighborhood during this time, large color, TVs were enviable, as they were not featured in all households. Fortunately, for them, the fruit of Marvin's labor made this a possibility - *there is that American Dream again!*

Nonetheless, it was Friday night- Pam was washing dishes, Melvin was in the kitchen talking on the phone, Marvin was napping in the bedroom and the younger Mack boys were sitting in front of the screen, "Indian style", prepared to indulge themselves in an episode of "Different Strokes". Just as the opening tunes played and the show credits began to run, Monte noticed a flash of light bounce off the glass panels of the entrance door. Before he could process the reflection and confirm his observation with Randy, he heard a loud bang that was initially mistaken for thunder; the downstairs door was kicked open followed by a voice yelling "POLICE!" and a collection of lights running up the steps, pushing through the glass paneled door. The boys were wide-eyed and frozen in place as flashlights and black shoes danced around their motionless bodies. Unsure of how to react to the sudden shift in events, Monte cried out, "MOMMY!" Randy was jolted by the sound of this distress signal and immediately assumed the role of 'protector', pulling Monte into a corner in an effort to shield him from the chaos. "We have a warrant…Where is Marvin? Where are the drugs?" a loud voice echoed from inside of their parent's bedroom. "What drugs?" Marvin replied calmly. Monte was terrified by the commotion but the combination of Randy's embrace and Marvin's serenity despite the hostility, was soothing.  Just as he gained courage to take a peak in the direction of the police officers, there was Pam, burrowing her way through the gauntlet of men gripping their flashlights with one hand and their pistols with the other.  The sight of Pam provided both Monte and Randy with a feeling of relief that only a mother can provide. "Get up, boys, we're going downstairs to Grandma Rose's apartment" As they made their way through the glass paneled door and down the very steps that were desecrated just moments before, Monte could hear the pubescent voice of Melvin saying, 'take your hands off of my father, PIGS!'.  When the door to Grandma Rose opened, Pam shoved the young boys into the vestibule and immediately ran back up to their second floor apartment to ensure the security of Marvin and Melvin.  If American history taught her anything, it was that police invasions on a Black residence often resulted in injury (or worse) on those occupying the space.  While on the first floor, in Grandma Rose's apartment, Monte could hear the sound of the men rummaging through rooms combined with the muffled demands of the officers towards Marvin.  The thumps of their footsteps rattled the photo frames in Rose's china cabinet as they echoed throughout the house. "What's going on, Grandma?" Randy asked in his elevated voice intended to accommodate Rose's bad hearing.  She responded in a similar volume, "It's nonsense, baby; your father has a certain reputation and sometimes there's a price to pay for the decisions we make" Monte and Randy looked at one another in confusion as her indirect response landed awkwardly on them. Realizing that her comments may have led to more questions than answers, she simply said, "just keep praying- Jesus is coming soon enough." Grandma Rose, like many of the other church-going elders at the time, saw Revelations in all events that were not be explained with logic: AIDS epidemic- "Jesus is coming"; snow on Easter- "Jesus is coming"; NWA album- "JESUS IS COMING"

Monte and Randy continued to listen to the muffled thumps from upstairs on Rose's popcorn ceiling and anxiously waited for the boots to exit their home with the same urgency as they entered moments before. Different Strokes was a distant memory, as all the boys could think about was the events taking place in their apartment.  "Hey, Randy, why does Melvin get to stay with Mommy and Daddy- and why did he call them pigs?" "Because he's the oldest, Fatboy, that's why…"  After some time, the voices softened and Monte began to hear the heavy footsteps retreating towards the entrance door and down the staircase to exit their home. He quickly ran to the front door to see if Marvin and/or Melvin were accompanying the officers and just as he pressed his small head against the mesh screen door, the pink face of the ringleader of these officers, Detective Hugo, met Monte. Hugo was whispering something in the ear of another officer when Monte's presence startled him.  "Hey little man, what's your name?" he said with a sinister grin. Despite what Hugo represented, Monte's gullibility kicked in as he began to nervously respond in kind- "M-m-my name is Monte" he said. "DON'T TALK TO STRANGERS, Fatboy!" Melvin interjected from the window above before the exchange between Hugo and Monte advanced any further.  Hugo chuckled lightly and winked at the Monte.  As he made his way towards his vehicle, he said, "maybe we'll meet again, Monte- see ya later" "FUCK YOU, Hugo!" Melvin yelled from the second floor window, as Hugo's caravan rolled off.

"HELLOOOO...what's taking so long?" Pam's voice boomed through the bathroom, pulling Marvin and Monte back from the depths of their memories and grounding them back to the present.  "Let's go!- Melvin is on the way out and judge needs to know that his family is here to support him."  As Marvin and Monte gathered themselves and prepared to exit the restroom, Marvin turned to his youngest son and softly declared, "My past will not define your future, Monte" In the moment, Monte acknowledged the gravity of the moment; however, he responded to Marvin's prophecy with his signature grin and a hint of cynicism- "only time will tell, *MONEY MARV*!" They embraced, glanced back into the mirror at one another and chuckled nervously as they walked out of the door and back into the courthouse lobby.

# MY BROTHER'S KEEPER, YOUR BROTHER'S REAPER

**At home, the Mack boys were sworn enemies** who playfully competed over everything from Mike Tyson's Punch-out Nintendo games, to who was the favorite son of Pam and Marvin. They played hard, loved hard and fought harder. Melvin was four years older than Randy was and Randy was four years older than Monte. However, the age gap between the boys was no exception.  Melvin showed no mercy on his younger brothers.  If there were any internal conflicts between them at home, the moment they walked out of the house, they were united and responsible for the safety and well-being of one another, unconditionally.  Marvin and Pam preached the importance of support and how loyalty, within their family, was the pillar to their relationship.  On the streets of Anderson, and within their neighborhood, as the runt of the Mack clan, Monte often benefited from the reputations of his older brothers as well as the alliances formed with their associates on Liberty Ave and beyond.

As an overweight kid with a speech impediment, access to a coalition of watchmen with documented 'street cred' was essential to Monte's survival.  Around town, he was affectionately known as 'Lil Bruh' and despite his village of guardians; Monte endeavored to navigate Anderson on his own terms just as the Mack men before him.  Unfortunately, this was virtually impossible because whenever he would venture outside of the designated boundaries of their block and onto Liberty Ave, he would hear "*Lil Bruh, where you goin'…Lil Bruh, get home…Lil*

*Bruh, keep walking…*" Unattended, Monte was permitted in select places.  There was *Harry's* for Jamaican beef patties, sugar cane, and king fish dinners; *Stop 1 Market* for snacks and C&C soda and *"The Stink Store"*, which was a local Bodega that featured a mini slaughterhouse and butcher at the rear of store, hence the reason for the nickname (*Stink* store).  Monte dreaded the Stink Store; however, if Stop 1 was out of butter crunch cookies, he would endure the aroma of raw meat if that meant getting his favorite snacks.

During late 1980s, early 90s, Liberty Ave was a microcosm of American society consisting of (illegal) trade, commerce, conflict and diplomacy and Melvin aka "Born Perfection", was an appointed ambassador who hated to see his baby brother on "the block". Consequently, if Melvin was not in sight, his friends acted as his proxy. It was the "god body" era of the Five Percent Nation and everyone within Melvin's inner circle adopted pseudonyms in lieu of their birth names. Beyond "Born Perfection", Monte's extended family consisted of "Father Divine" "King Intelligent", "Knowledge", and "Understanding"- these young men were among Liberty Ave's early guardians and in Monte's opinion, they were some of coolest people around.  While Melvin protected Monte on and around Liberty Ave, Randy was the enforcer everywhere else. When it came to his younger brother's safety, Randy was unforgiving and non-negotiable.  In some ways, Randy felt personally responsible for Monte despite teasing and chastising him frequently.  There were many instances where Randy Mack transformed into "*Randy Savage*" on behalf of Monte; however, it was a second grade encounter with the class bully that is most memorable…

# MOVE SOMETHIN'

Before his transfer to Glen Park, while attending their local public school, PS #21, Monte kept a low profile. Despite being a shy kid, his personality did not command the room in the same way Melvin and Randy did. However, he remained known by the older students as 'Lil Bruh'.  Growing up, Monte idolized Melvin aka Born for his style and fashion sense and wanted nothing more than to dress like his older brother.

Understanding that Melvin, at the tender age of 16, had gainful employment on Liberty Ave, Monte begged him to buy a shiny Starter jacket similar to those worn by Uncle Luke and the 2 Live Crew in the 'Move Somethin' video, because Pam refused to spend the money.  It was the fall of second grade and as a gift for Monte's birthday and earning good grades on his first term report card; Melvin surprised him with a walk to Carlo's clothing store. Carlo's was a bodega turned micro department store that was located a few blocks away on Broadway. This storefront boutique appealed to drug dealers because it offered convenience.  Furthermore, where else could you get custom Clark's Wallabies and Britisher moccasins outside of Harlem? Carlo's was an Anderson staple and Monte finally had the opportunity to shop there- he was too excited for his own good- he was unable to remove the smile from his face as he walked alongside Melvin.

When they arrived at the store, several of Melvin's friends from other blocks who were also there to shop greeted them. "Is that Lil Bruh?" One of the teenagers asked. "Yea, man he's been a good kid so I wanted to get him fresh for school" Monte was beaming with pride listening to his big brother boast on his accomplishments. One of Melvin's friends, with the gold rope necklace and crisp white t-shirt, reached into his pocket, thumbed through a roll of dollar bills and in response said "take this Lil Bruh and keep being a good kid" as he handed Monte a ten dollar bill.  For a moment, Monte was torn; he thought to himself *"why would I stay in school when these guys are clearly living the dream?"* However, fear of disappointing his family quickly killed those thoughts.  At any rate, this was shaping out to be the best day ever.  Melvin's friends exited the store as he and Monte began to peruse Carlo's. "Pick out whatever you want but it can't be too expensive", said Melvin. That was music to Monte's ears because he knew exactly what he wanted– Uncle Luke's emerald green University of Miami Hurricanes jacket! Pushing through the garments on the rack, Monte was dismayed to find that the coveted Hurricanes jacket was nonexistent.  Observing the disappointment in Monte's face, Melvin approached Carlo's wife at the counter and after a brief chat, he returned to Monte to inform him that the jacket was unavailable.  Before Monte could drop his head in disappointment, Melvin snatched a black and red Louisville

Cardinals jacket from the hanger and quickly paired it with black high top Reebok 5411s and said, "Check it out, Fats- if you get this jacket, you can get the sneakers to match!" Melvin was spending more money in an attempt to offer his baby brother some consolation when in actuality, the time and attention that he was spending was sufficient for Monte. Nevertheless, Monte accepted the generous offer because he knew well enough that declining the gift would be *blocking his blessings*, even if they were gifts purchased with "dirty money"- there goes that *American Dream*, again.

Gripping the royal blue Carlo's shopping bag, Monte marched home alongside Melvin with purpose- shoulders back, head held high and a pattern to his step that was reminiscent of "George Jefferson". Melvin observed his bolt of confidence but reserved his comments to allow Monte to savor the feeling. Of course, his moment in the sun was short lived as soon as they reached Liberty Ave and Randy speeding by on a "borrowed" red GT bicycle with white mag wheels. "Hey Fatboy, what's in the bag, Carlo's sells husky size now?" "Leave him alone *Randy*- he earned it" Melvin replied on Monte's behalf. Randy rolled his eyes, turned the bike upright into a "wheelie" and continued riding.

That evening, Monte carefully draped his jacket across the bed, and then added a bright red sweatshirt and baggy black sweatpants atop it, creating a fashionable contrast of colors and textures with his Reeboks. That night felt like Christmas Eve as Monte anticipated getting dressed for school and the reaction his outfit would garner from his second grade classmates, especially Laura Dennis, the prettiest girl in class.

Morning arrived and the sun was shining brighter than ever.  Monte woke up without the assistance of Pam and to his surprise- he woke up with dry sheets- *"this is the day that the Lord has made…"* echoed in his head.  He quickly ran to the bathroom to take a shower so that he could allocate his excess time to "get fresh".  Before getting dressed, he glanced into the living room, where Melvin slept and said softly, **'Thanks Mel'**.

The moment of truth was upon him- he was preparing to get dressed but before putting on his first layer, he had to apply extra deodorant- Tussy cream was his antiperspirant of choice; however, he could never avoid getting the cream stuck within his fingernails.  This morning was atypical so Monte made sure to wash his hands to ensure that he did not stain the satin material of his Starter jacket- *"Don't get this shit dirty!"* were Melvin's instructions when the jacket was purchased just the day before.  Randy had a proclivity for sarcasm but observing the confidence displayed by Monte after he assembled his outfit left Randy speechless.

At school, the response Monte received from his peers was just as he imagined it would be.  His morning was great and lunch was flawless as he managed not to stain his clothes while eating a sloppy Joe sandwich. Because Monte felt like a baby boss that day, he decided to forgo playing during recess and instead walked the playground perimeter.  As he crossed the basketball courts where most of his friends congregated, he heard the soft, angelic voice of Laura Dennis say "Hi, Monte- nice jacket" Monte almost fainted!  Tussy was no match for his body temperature as he began to sweat and breathe heavily. "Th th thank you!" managed to escape his lips as he smiled from ear-to-ear.  Laura responded in kind with a smile of her own and Monte was in love. It was a brief moment that he assumed was shared by just he and Laura until he looked up and noticed the class bully, Stanley aka "Stacks', peering at him with disgust.  Recognizing Stacks' displeasure with his catching the attention of Laura, Monte attempted to disarm him with the proverbial head nod that in Anderson, translated to "What's up, bro?"; however, given the tension that he felt from Stacks, Monte's head nod was more of a non-threatening *"hello neighbor"* gesture.

Monte was certainly not a punk but thanks to the training of his older brothers, he possessed a keen ability to avoid trouble when it loomed on the horizon.  Stacks failed to reply in kind, much to Monte's chagrin.  Instead, Stacks punched the palm of his left hand with his right fist and said "after school- me and you, fat ass!" The playground fell silent by Stacks' declaration of war and all eyes were on Monte in anticipation of his rebuttal. The butterflies in his gut that previously fluttered for Laura were now fighting as his anxiety level began to skyrocket- the Tussy was non-existent at this point and all Monte could think about was sweating through his sweatshirt onto his new jacket.  He replied to Stacks with a nonchalant shoulder shrug as to say *"whatever"*. Monte's nonverbal response only enraged Stacks further because it invoked a harmonious chorus of *"oooooooh"* from their classmates. Monte was beside himself but it was too late; he could only hope for Stacks to find Jesus or detained by the cops before dismissal- the latter scenario was more likely than the former.

For the next three hours, Monte reflected on the sequence of events that led to him having to fight Stacks at dismissal. The best day ever had taken an ominous turn, leaving Monte unable to shake the feeling that his current circumstances were somehow a consequence of his own actions. The sound of the dismissal bell signaled that it was "game time". For Monte, it was *do or die-* literally! In the Mack household, Pam and Marvin had a golden rule: *if you do not defend yourself outside of the house, you better be prepared to defend yourself when you get home.* Defeat accompanied by a valiant effort was more favorable than no effort at all because if his family learned that he did not fight back, he would surely have to fight them all upon his arrival back home. "One ass whipping is always better than four" was Monte's approach to street fighting.

Before the exit doors opened, Monte's eyes raced across the corridor searching for Randy so that he could walk home under the protective custody of his brother. When he was unable to locate Randy. He did his best to go undetected by blending in with the crowd of older students filing out of the building. Unfortunately, his gift was now a curse- he was easily recognizable by the shiny, black and red jacket.  The moment he stepped foot outside of the school, someone pushed him from behind onto the dirty pavement. He picked himself up and before plucking the glass from his palms, he inspected his jacket to confirm that it was still clean.  "We don't have to fight each other!" Monte beseeched as he back peddled away from his Stacks. "Too late, fat ass! You think you're cool with your new outfit, huh?" Just as Monte began to plead his case, someone pushed him forward, inadvertently bumping into Stacks and knocking him to the ground. Students gasped in disbelief before they began to cheer for Monte, the unlikely underdog- *'FIGHT-FIGHT-FIGHT!'* they yelled.  Monte wanted to relish the moment so he used this unexpected advantage to his benefit and began to throw punches towards Stacks as he laid on the concrete...

The crowd grew larger and cheered louder and just as Monte was beginning to imagine his victory lap, he felt an aggressive tug on his left arm and assumed it was a concerned teacher intervening to break up the fight. Before he knew it, his right arm held as well and he soon realized that an unknown person who was clearly there to aid Stacks was restraining him. Neutralized, Monte could only see the shoes of this mystery assailant- he wore yellow and blue Nike Cortez sneakers and though Monte was impressed with his style, he was preoccupied with trying to free himself from the "full Nelson" hold suddenly placed on him.

Monte exerted so much energy during his brief rally that he was exhausted and unable to release himself. Despite being fatigued and helpless because of the double team attack, Monte held his head high and eagerly scanned the playground for a familiar face. He looked beyond the cheering students and in the distance; he could see Randy walking with a group of friends. "RANDY, HELP ME!" he desperately screeched. As everyone shifted attention towards the direction of Randy who was down the street, the mystery individual holding onto Monte said, "Oh shit -

hit him!" Stacks punched Monte in the face and the grips holding his arms instantly released.  Falling to the ground with blood in his mouth, he was only able to catch a glimpse of the blue and yellow Nikes running in the opposite direction.  The crowd dispersed and Monte laid on the pavement, in dramatic fashion, awaiting Randy's rescue.  It was a fifteen-second wait but it felt like fifteen years and when his big brother helped him to his feet, he burst into tears as Randy brushed the dirt from his new jacket and picked pebbles from his hair.  Randy was furious- "who did this to you? POINT THEM OUT!" Monte's lips were moving but his response was inaudible due to his hysteria.  "Stop crying, fat boy and speak!" Monte was reluctant to disclose the identity of his perpetrators because he knew his brother better than anyone did and the wrath of Randy was relentless.

Randy was prepared to scorch elementary school Earth in defense of Monte because he felt that his negligent supervision left his brother vulnerable. Furthermore, Pam and Marvin would definitely view Monte's 'beat down' as a reflection of Randy because it occurred on his watch.  From Randy's perspective, payback was imminent.

Monte picked up his bag and walked slowly towards Liberty Ave with Randy as he explained the chain of events that led to the fight with Stacks.

Despite the defeat, Randy was proud of Monte's ability to defend himself and disturbingly, happy to report this to his parents.  Fortunately, Pam and Marvin dismissed the encounter as childhood growing pains.  However, Melvin responded with a simple question, "Y'all scared?" Randy resented the inquiry but assured Melvin that fear was not a factor- on the other hand, Monte begged to differ. Nevertheless, the details surrounding the mystery person were unsettling to both boys but Randy was determined to get revenge on everyone responsible for Monte's tears.

The next morning, the boys walked to school as normal and on the way there, Randy promised Monte that he would handle his problems. Upon reaching the playground, before students lined up with their respective teachers, Randy and Monte ran into Randy's best friend and underboss, *"Batman"*.  He had a baby face and known to everyone, even adults, as Batman- no one knew his real name. Batman said, "Let's go- we caught them!" They followed Batman to the side of the building and as they turned the corner, Monte recognized Stacks lying on the ground next to a slightly older student wearing the elusive blue and yellow Nike Cortez sneakers. The Nikes belonged to Kory, Stacks' older cousin who, ironically, complimented Monte on his jacket the day before. Randy wasted no time punching and kicking Stacks and Kory before ordering them both to stand up."Y'all jumped my little brother and thought I was going to let it slide?" Randy asked. Before they muttered a response - *POW!* - Randy punched Kory to the ground and Batman proceeded to stomp on him.  Randy turned to Monte and directed him to get his revenge.  Feeling pity for the boys, Monte was hesitant.

Sensing his reservation, Randy invoked the Mack household's self-defense decree and reminded Monte *"one ass whipping is always better than four"*.  Reluctantly, Monte joined Randy and Batman in the punishment of their temporary detainees.  Though he was cautious about igniting an ongoing feud with Stacks, Randy's action provided Monte with an added sense of security.

As class began, Stacks solemnly approached Monte's desk. With a clenched fist, he extended his hand and just as Monte's physical response began to debate "fight or flight", Stacks said, "I'm sorry, man-peace" and gently tapped his fist against Monte's knuckles, giving him a "pound". Monte responded in kind with "peace" as Stacks made his way to his desk.

Later that night, seeking redemption, Randy and Monte shared their triumph with Melvin.  After overhearing this interaction, Pam began to brainstorm on how to provide her sons with opportunities beyond shiny coats and schoolyard scuffles.  Four weeks later, they transferred to Glen Park's school district. After Monte left PS #21 for Glen Park, the next time he saw Stacks was in juvenile court, while he was accompanying Pam and Randy.  Stacks was accompanied by his lawyer.

# SUMMER MADNESS

**In Anderson, NJ**, during the early 1990s, summertime was a cherished period that all of the kids on Monte's block enjoyed. Monte, along with his small group of friends, could not afford summer vacations so if they were not attending the occasional day camp, they were home, and left to their own devices- waking up past noon and eating ramen noodles until their parents arrived home from work.

For Monte, summer 1991 was highly anticipated because Pam agreed to enroll him into the Anderson City Boys and Girls Club summer camp. Both Melvin and Randy had attended the program in the past where they allowed swimming lessons, bumper pool tournaments and field trips to provide an escape from the summer heat of the streets. Randy has since discovered alternate activities to occupy his free time. These days, the allure of the financial opportunities presented by the commerce on Liberty Ave preoccupied the older Mack boys. As such, Monte was without proper supervision and the Boys Club was the best option. In Monte's opinion, Pam could rest assured that he was supervised during the day and in the worst-case scenario, he would potentially lose some weight- this was a longshot but he was free to dream!

It was mid-July and summer was off to an outstanding start. Monte was enjoying the best of both worlds- summer camp by day and tag with his friends by night. Beyond that, he even had the privilege of attending a few neighborhood cookouts- one of his favorite summer pastimes. However, as summer progressed, so did the climate. Monte appreciated the summer heat but if the temperature was too high, he'd begin sweating through his clothes. He accepted being the "fat kid" but the "sweaty fat kid" was a nonstarter.

On this particular day, the heat was expected to reach 95 degrees and despite Monte's urge to remain in bed under the warm, but cooling, breeze of the dusty square window fan, he got dressed for camp because it was pizza lunch day.  Stepping over Melvin's pile of old Spotbilt sneakers littered across the floor, Monte made his way to the bathroom to take a bath only to learn that there was no more hot water available.  Due to his frequent bedwetting, a lack of hot water would typically be detrimental to Monte but today, he surprisingly woke up slightly damp. Furthermore, he welcomed the cold shower in hopes that it would offset the heat and cool him down a bit.

"Monte, let's go!" Pam yelled from the driver's side of her maroon Hyundai Excel as she manually rolled down the window and sweat beads rolled down her left arm.  The heat was unbearable and Pam's frustration level was beginning to peak before she reached work.  Monte scurried down the steps and got into the car just as Pam prepared to leave him behind.  During the drive to camp, Monte stared out of the window and imagined how his cousin, Wilson, was doing.  Wilson's mother was Grandma Maxine's baby sister making him Pam's first cousin and Monte's second cousin.  However, given that Wilson was only one year older than Monte, they had a very close relationship.  Wilson lived on the north side of Anderson with his mother and grandmother, who was Monte's great-grandmother. They were devout Christians who ran a tight shift.  Given the mischief that typically occurred within the Mack house, Wilson did not visit Monte often; however, Monte was allowed to have sleepovers at Wilson's from time to time. Despite the strict rules that accompanied visiting Wilson's house, Monte enjoyed playing age-appropriate games and having age-appropriate chats with his favorite cousin.  However, the relationship was mutually beneficial.  For example, Monte would often smuggle cassette tapes of the most recent hip-hop songs for he and Wilson to listen to when no one was around.

Monte was scheduled to sleepover Wilson's after camp and imagining his visit was a temporary distraction from the heat that radiated throughout the car.

Upon reaching the Boys Club, Monte was greeted by the pungent aroma of chlorine deriving from the swimming pool located in the basement.  Rubbing his burning eyes, he signed in just in time to grab the last juice box.  Except for having pizza for lunch, the day was underwhelming- Monte participated in a Nintendo tournament, played ten rounds of "duck-duck-goose!" and watched music videos in the lounge where 'Summertime' by Fresh Prince played at least ten times.

As dismissal drew near, Monte's anticipation grew, his eyes fixed on the lobby entrance, eagerly awaiting Pam's arrival. Only then could he go home and pack for his weekend fun at Wilson's.

But Pam was late- "where is she?," Monte thought.

He was beginning to grow anxious and this anxiety initiated his nerves, sending him into the restroom.  Sitting in the bathroom stall, the cold seat pressed against his legs, Monte thought of excuses for Pam's tardiness; "perhaps there was traffic" or "maybe she stopped at the Italian bakery near camp to surprise me with a cannoli," he thought.  Just as he was beginning to accept his surprise cannoli theory, he heard a deep voice over the PA system say, "Monte Mack- your ride is here!" he stood up so fast that he almost forgot to flush the toilet. He washed his hands and ran to the lobby with wet hands to greet Pam (and his cannoli) but Pam was not there.  Instead, it was Luisa, Melvin's girlfriend who was rumored to be pregnant.

"Why are you here?" Monte curiously inquired.  "Let's go, the taxi is waiting", Luisa replied, dismissing Monte's question. Once outside, Monte asked again- "what the hell Is going on, Luisa- is my mother OK?" Luisa's eyes filled with tears as she spoke- "Miss Pam is fine; she's downtown, at the police station, with Melvin- he was arrested today" The delivery of this news sent Monte's mind into a tailspin. He imagined his older brother seated in a cold, dark room handcuffed to a steel chair positioned under a single light bulb that swayed back and forth suspended from a wire.  Keenly aware of his brother's occupation, Monte did not have to imagine the reason for Melvin's arrest but the news came at an unexpected inconvenience to his family. Melvin's arrest meant that Monte's visit to Wilson's house was likely canceled as Luisa instructed him to stay with Randy and Grandma Rose until Pam and Marvin arrived home, hopefully with Melvin in tow.

It was hot as hell and beyond the disappointment of not visiting Wilson or getting a cannoli, Monte had to stay in Grandma Rose's air conditioner-less apartment.  The floors of Rose's apartment were covered with a brown shag carpet that absorbed heat and camouflaged roaches equally.  The big screen television in Grandma Rose's living room did not work so Monte's options were limited. He was left with the dilemma of watching the New York Yankees baseball game with Rose in her bedroom or stare out of the window and watch his friends play tag while pushing their young bodies to the brink of heat exhaustion– he opted for the window seat.

Monte was anxious as he peered out of the window because he desperately wanted his parents to come home. He wanted to go outside to play; Randy was nowhere to be found and without proper supervision, Monte was not allowed to go out.  Just as he began to give up hope, Monte noticed a stream of water running alongside of the curb towards the sewer at the end of the block.  Before he could react, he heard a loud cheer as kids ran towards the center of the block. He pressed his face against the sticky glass window for a better view of the commotion and to his surprise, the fire hydrant was open!

During the summer, it was a common occurrence to see children cooling themselves off with fire hydrant water; however, the older residents on Monte's block despised this activity because of the decrease in water pressure and periods of rusty sink water households were forced to endure as a result.  Today's heat was no exception, but someone was brave enough to offer the neighborhood kids some temporary free fun and give every car that dared to pass by a free wash.

Monte was beside himself because there was no sign of Randy until he suddenly emerged shirtless and soaking wet clutching a 2-foot long hydrant wrench in his hand. 'Fatboy, hurry come get in the water pump before the cops come!' Apparently, Randy was the brave soul who opened the fire hydrant.

Monte quickly jumped up, kicked off his shoes and bolted through Rose's front door to join everyone in the water. In the back of his mind, he knew that Pam would not approve of his participation but he was with Randy so technically he was under supervision. Besides, with Melvin's quagmire, *"Mommy has bigger fish to fry"* Monte thought to himself as the cold water splashed his shirt and ricocheted onto the pavement creating a temporary rainbow.

Monte's feelings of disappointment in missing Wilson's sleepover were fleeting as he basked in the water play with Randy and other neighborhood children.  It was so hot that even a few of Melvin's friends from Liberty Ave came by the fire hydrant to cool off.  Though they were more interested in keeping their sneakers from getting wet, they appreciated the temporary reprieve from the heat. As Monte stood on the curb to wait for a passing car to drive by, one of Melvin's friends said, "Hey, Lil Bruh- did Born get out yet?"  Monte shrugged his shoulders in uncertainty but he was annoyed because the young man's inquiry was a reminder that Melvin was arrested a few hours earlier. Monte rushed back near the hydrant and dipped his head into the flowing water as if he was attempting to drown his anxiety over his current family situation.  As he lifted his head from the water and cleared his eyes, he could see red

and blue lights in the distance just as the crowd of his
fellow participants began to demonstrate their displeasure
in seeing law enforcement with a harmonious "Boooo".
"Let those kids enjoy themselves!" an adult woman shouted
from her front porch. "I'm sorry but we received several
complaints from some of your neighbors," the young
officer replied.  "But it's hot as hell, officer! What the fuck
are we supposed to, kill each other?"  Realizing that this
defiant retort was coming from Randy, Monte dropped his
head and began to run towards his older brother to calm
him down.  Unfortunately, Monte's demands were
ineffective as his voice was forced to compete with the
tunes of "Summertime" blaring from the handheld boom
box that sat near Randy.

Their parents already had one son in handcuffs; they could
not handle another– at least not today.  Monte reached
Randy just as the officer approached him. 'It's no problem,
sir- my brother is just irritated by the heat, don't arrest him
PLEASE!" Monte raised his head to look at the officer and
as they locked eyes, Monte recognized him from Hugo's
"Friday Night Lights" raid.  Apparently, he recognized
Monte as well because he adjusted his tone and level of

aggression as he said, "we're just doing our jobs, kid".  As the officer walked back towards the water hydrant, Monte shoved Randy and said, "Are you crazy? Don't get us in trouble…AGAIN!"  Randy dismissed his younger brother with a middle finger and walked away.  The neighborhood fun was short-lived but for Monte and Randy, it provided a much-needed distraction from both the heat and the myriad problems that were defining his day up until that time.

An hour later, Pam and Marvin returned home with Melvin and the looks on their faces were alarming. Pam was humming softly, Melvin wore a blank stare but the rapid movement of his eyes indicated that his mind was racing at one hundred miles per hour. Monte and Randy quietly debated about what Melvin was pondering as he sat at the kitchen table in silence- "I think he's mad because his sneakers are ruined", Monte whispered. "No, silly! He's probably thinking about the money he lost when the cops arrested him- *he's not getting that back*" Randy sarcastically replied.

In an attempt to offer some consolation, Monte approached Melvin as he sulked, presumably pondering his dirty sneakers and/or his financial woes. Unfortunately, before the greetings escaped Monte's mouth, Marvin's baritone voice intervened- "he's dealing with grown man business, Monte- keep moving and leave him alone" Bewildered by Marvin's interruption combined with his uncharacteristic display of frustration, Monte was frozen in place for a moment until Melvin gifted him with a slight grin and a wink.  Despite the gravity of Melvin's situation, his brief, non-verbal communication provided Monte with temporary comfort. Heeding to Marvin's command, Monte kept moving until he reached the refrigerator- all of the stress and heat was making him hungry- again.

As Monte opened the freezer compartment to allow the freon-laced cold mist emitting from the frost to cool him down, Pam entered the kitchen appearing defeated and deflated.  "Ma, are you ok?" He asked softly. "Yes, baby-everything is fine" she replied. In an attempt to relieve her of the burden of preparing dinner, Monte decided to prepare his own meal. Reaching his arm into the cabinet, he grabbed a ramen noodle brick.  Pam preferred that he consumed something a bit more nutritious; however, today was exceptional. She overlooked both his meal choice and the fact that his clothes were soaked as she walked out of the kitchen leaving him with only a superficial safety reminder- "be careful and don't burn the house down, baby"

Perplexed by Pam's unorthodox behavior; Monte reserved sharing his fire hydrant experience with her- 'she has enough on her mind' he thought to himself.  The remainder of the night was equally awkward– the record player was silent, Melvin paced the floor, and Pam was on the phone all night trying to make sense of the circumstances surrounding Melvin.  Meanwhile, the smoke that filled the air from Marvin's Newport cigarette was pervasive.  Monte and Randy did everything in their power to stay out of sight—everything except retreating downstairs to Grandma Rose's apartment, as that was an absolute last resort.

Monte was pleased that Melvin was not in jail but the atmosphere within the Mack household was a bit ominous. He laid down on the bottom bunk with the intention of paying Melvin a visit after he parents went to sleep but instead, shut his eyes and dozed off in his wet clothes.

Monte was in a deep sleep when he was awakened by what he can only describe as a wet tickle in his right ear. Growing up the baby of the house, Monte was the recipient of his fair share of 'wet willies" however this was a different and a bit more invasive.  Dazed and confused, Monte laid motionless for a few seconds to verify that this was not a dream- *"What the fuck is that?"* he thought.  The darkness of the room made this encounter all the more eerie. It was as if the world paused and all other sounds vanished- he was alone with his thoughts and the mystery sensation that was in his head.

Monte recalled his earlier water play in the fire hydrant and assumed that the feeling was the water draining from his ear. Just as he was about to tilt his head in an attempt to accelerate the release of the water from his head, the tickles became more intense and he had his answer- *"GODDAMMIT"* he yelled, startling Randy and awaking Pam and Marvin, who nervously came running to his aid. Marvin was visibly enraged- but, following the day he had with Melvin, Monte accepted his father's disposition. "What's wrong baby, you wet the bed again?" Pam asked.

At this point, Monte was panicking as he yelled back,

**'MOMMY, I THINK I HAVE A ROACH IN MY EAR'**

Randy stood to his feet in disbelief and inquired, "How did you manage to do that, Fatboy?"  The boys had prior encounters with the filthy insects from finding them in cereal boxes to inadvertently transporting them to school in their backpacks; however, a roach in the ear was a Mack family first.

Fed up and frustrated, Marvin grabbed Monte by the arm and led him into the bathroom.  Once there, he turned the light on only to see additional roaches scurry across the floor tiles to escape.  In an act of desperation, Marvin tilted Monte's head downwards but when gravity failed to discharge the creature, Marvin resorted to force and began gently banging Monte's head with the ball of his hand. This was completely ineffective and only made matters worse because it agitated the roach, causing it to move faster in Monte's ear and deeper into his head.

Pam jumped into action and ran into the bathroom with her purse and car keys- 'let's go to the emergency room!' stepping over Melvin and Luisa, who were asleep on the living room floor, Monte and Pam rushed out the glass-paneled door and down the front steps.  As the car screeched out of the driveway, Randy, now wide awake but still perplexed, glanced in the direction of Marvin and said "this shit is wild, Pops" Marvin took a deep drag from his Newport cigarette and simply replied "it can be worse, son".

The Macks resided in Anderson however, whenever there was a need for a non-life threatening ER visit, Pam would drive the distance to Glen Park's Valley Hospital as opposed to Anderson's Barnert Hospital, which was only five minutes away.  Beyond the quality of care, service in the suburbs was consistently more prompt than in the inner city.  In fact, Pam delivered Melvin and Randy at Barnert, but the convenience led her to give birth to Monte at Valley—another factor that was subject to his older brothers' teasing.

Interestingly enough, on this day, Monte would have preferred to see a local physician because by all accounts, Barnert's ER was likely more familiar with roach extractions than Valley staff.

Upon arrival at Valley, valet service and a security guard, whose appearance reminded Monte of DJ Ralph McDaniels of Video Music Box, met them. While at the security desk, Pam was questioned about Monte's condition and if she has health insurance to afford care.  Despite the level or urgency, she wanted to remain discreet so she quietly said, "my son has a bug in his ear".  The security glanced at the grimace on Monte's face, raised his eyebrow and leaned in to whisper, "no offense but when you say that your son has a bug in his ear, do you mean a roach?" Pam replied with a prideful response underscored by shame as she said 'Yes, a roach- does the bug type determine the level of service that we receive?'  Pam took the security guard aback yet, given the circumstances, it was understandable.  The security guard replied, "In fact, it does make a difference; if a roach is in his ear, your son will become a priority." Turning towards Monte, who, by this time was on the brink of crying, the guard continued with empathy "Don't worry, little man- I had a roach in my ear before" The security guard's confession provided Pam and Monte with the assurance and solidarity that they desperately needed.

In light of the circumstances, Monte's ER intake was expedited. After he explained how he spent time near the fire hydrant, the nurse informed Monte that the easiest way to remove the roach from his ear would be to squirt additional fluid to flush it out. When she returned to the room holding a large syringe filled with a clear liquid, Monte grabbed Pam's hand and squeezed it tightly.  The nurse began injecting the fluid into his ear canal and as it traveled through Monte's head, it felt as if the critter was rapidly dancing on his brain. This itch was impossible to scratch and it was driving him crazy! Suddenly, the dancing stopped. Monte assumed that the roach was released until he overheard the nurse mutter *"oh no"*. Concerned by the nurse's reaction, Pam asked, "What happened?" "It appears that the roach is lodged too deep within his ear and instead of pushing it out with the fluid, we drowned it"

No longer composed, Pam snarled, 'bitch, there is a dead roach in my son's ear?' This tone of voice and language was out of character for Pam but given the day she had with Melvin, the compounded stress of the events had taken a toll on her.  Monte was now becoming more agitated as he feared the thought of a roach corpse on his brain.  The nurse rushed from the room to page a doctor and escape the wrath of Pam.  Within two minutes, a tall man with a British accent, wearing a long white coat and surgical mask entered the room. "Hello, young man- so you have a cockroach in your ear- don't worry, we'll take good care of you"  He then turned to Pam and softly said "Mum, i understand your frustration but everything will be just fine"  Pam allowed the doctor's reassurance to allay her concerns but he was far from truly *understanding* how she felt in that moment.

To remove the insect, the doctor used very long surgical scissors that were curved at the tip.  The sight of the instrument was intimidating to Monte but the doctor's calm approach comforted him.  The procedure was prolonged because the roach was removed piece-by-piece; however, it was painless.  By the time it was all over, Pam was even chuckling at the doctor's dry jokes. 'All done, young man- the critter is no longer a tenant in your ear and you are good to go"

Exiting the emergency room, Monte was relieved but Pam was exhausted.  Before getting into the car, Monte took a moment to acknowledge the birds chirping and the color of the sky reflecting off the rising sun as daylight broke through the clouds.  "The clouds look like rainbow sherbet," he said. It humored Pam that Monte was thinking of food despite all of the ups and downs that they experienced in the past 24 hours. However, she found peace in his innocence. She smiled back at him, but before she knew it, tears began to fall from her face. "Ma, I'm sorry—I'll never play by the fire hydrant again, I promise," he pleaded

"It's not your fault, baby. I'm just tired."

"Tired of what?" he asked.

She thought for a moment and simply replied, "Circumstance."

They got into the car and drove off.

Several hours later, that afternoon, the heat was just as unbearable as the previous day and once again, someone opened the fire hydrant to allow the neighborhood to cool off temporarily.  Despite the urging of his friends to participate, Monte was disinterested, fearing another roach episode.  Instead, he remained near his front porch and watched the water stream past his driveway into the sewer. As he watched the kids run while soaked in water, he noticed a familiar car approaching his house- it was Grandma Maxine!

He jumped from the steps and ran towards the car to greet her.  While sitting in the driver's seat, Grandma Maxine noticed Monte trotting towards her, drenched in sweat. As he approached, smiling, she rolled down her window, releasing a cloud of cigarette smoke. Maxine bypassed the pleasantries and asked, "Do you want me to help you lose weight, baby?"  "OK, Grandma Maxine- let's do it!" he replied with a nervous yet hopeful smile.  **To be continued…**

# WALK WITH ME

### Epilogue:

As the sun sets over the bustling streets of Anderson, New Jersey, the lives of the Mack boys continue to unfold with each story woven into the vibrant tapestry of their community. As their lives continue, we catch fleeting glimpses of the characters who have journeyed through trials and triumphs, now navigating the complexities of adolescence and young adulthood. Through moments of laughter, reflection, and resilience, they confront new challenges and embrace their roles as brothers, sons, friends, and fathers.

These snapshots not only reveal their growth but also hint at the adventures yet to come, as their paths intertwine in the ever-evolving landscape of their lives. The journey is far from over; it's just beginning.

**YOUR SKIN IS YOUR WIN, NOT YOUR SIN**:  As Monte navigates his sense of belonging in the Glen Park and Anderson communities, he often finds himself seeking acceptance in environments where he feels alienated.

However, the comfort of Grandma Maxine and Pam's constant guidance and encouragement serves as his compass and constant reminder of the value and the beauty of being unapologetically Black.

**DON'T SWEAT THE TECHNIQUE**: As Randy's reckless behavior spirals out of control, a high-speed police chase in a stolen car forces him to confront his choices and gain much-needed perspective. Will he seize this opportunity to change his path?

**LOVE'S GONNA GET YA:** Melvin embraces the gift and challenge of parenting as he strives to balance street life with his responsibilities as a teenage father. This new family dynamic tests the limits of the Mack village, yet their commitment to "family" remains unwavering

h. monte: village ghetto land

# ABOUT THE AUTHOR

H. Monte is a product of his environment. With his heart and soul deeply connected to the experiences that shaped his perspective, he remains proximate to his community by celebrating it through storytelling. Drawing inspiration from lived experiences and the individuals who influenced his journey, he employs a fictional approach to explore the complexities of his family dynamic while honoring the strength gained by the struggles and setbacks endured by his family.

What started as a therapeutic outlet during daily commutes on public transportation evolved into a medium for H. Monte to stay connected to his past while navigating the present, giving rise to the ***Village Ghettoland*** chronicles.